FORT WORTH PUBLIC LIBRARY
3 1668 04288 3949
W9-BMY-203
PICTURE BOOKS MACLENNAN
2007
MacLennan, Cathy
Chicky chicky chook chook
East Regional 04/27/2010
EAST REGIONAL

For Lorraine
C.M.

First American edition published in 2007
by Boxer Books Limited.

Distributed in the United States and Canada by
Sterling Publishing Co., Inc.
387 Park Avenue South, New York, NY 10016-8810

First published in Great Britain in 2007
by Boxer Books Limited.
www.boxerbooks.com

Library of Congress Cataloging-in-Publication Data available.

ISBN-13: 978-1-905417-40-7
ISBN-10: 1-905417-40-3

5 7 9 10 8 6 4

Printed in China

Chicky Chicky Chook Chook

Cathy MacLennan

Boxer Books

Chicky, chicky, chook chook.
Chick, chick chick.

Chicky, chicky, chook chook,

peck...peck...pick.

Fizzy, fizzy, buzz buzz,

fizz, fizz buzz.

Fizzy, fizzy, buzz buzz,
busy...
busy...
buzzzzzz.

Kitty, kitty, kit cat.
Skit, skit scat.

Kitty, kitty, kit cat,

skit…skit…scatter.

Sunny, sunny, warm shine.
Sunnier.
Hot...
HOT

Sunny, sunny yellow shine.
Hotter.
hot...
TER.

Sunny, sunny, hot shine.

Snuggle, snuggle,
sleepy shine.

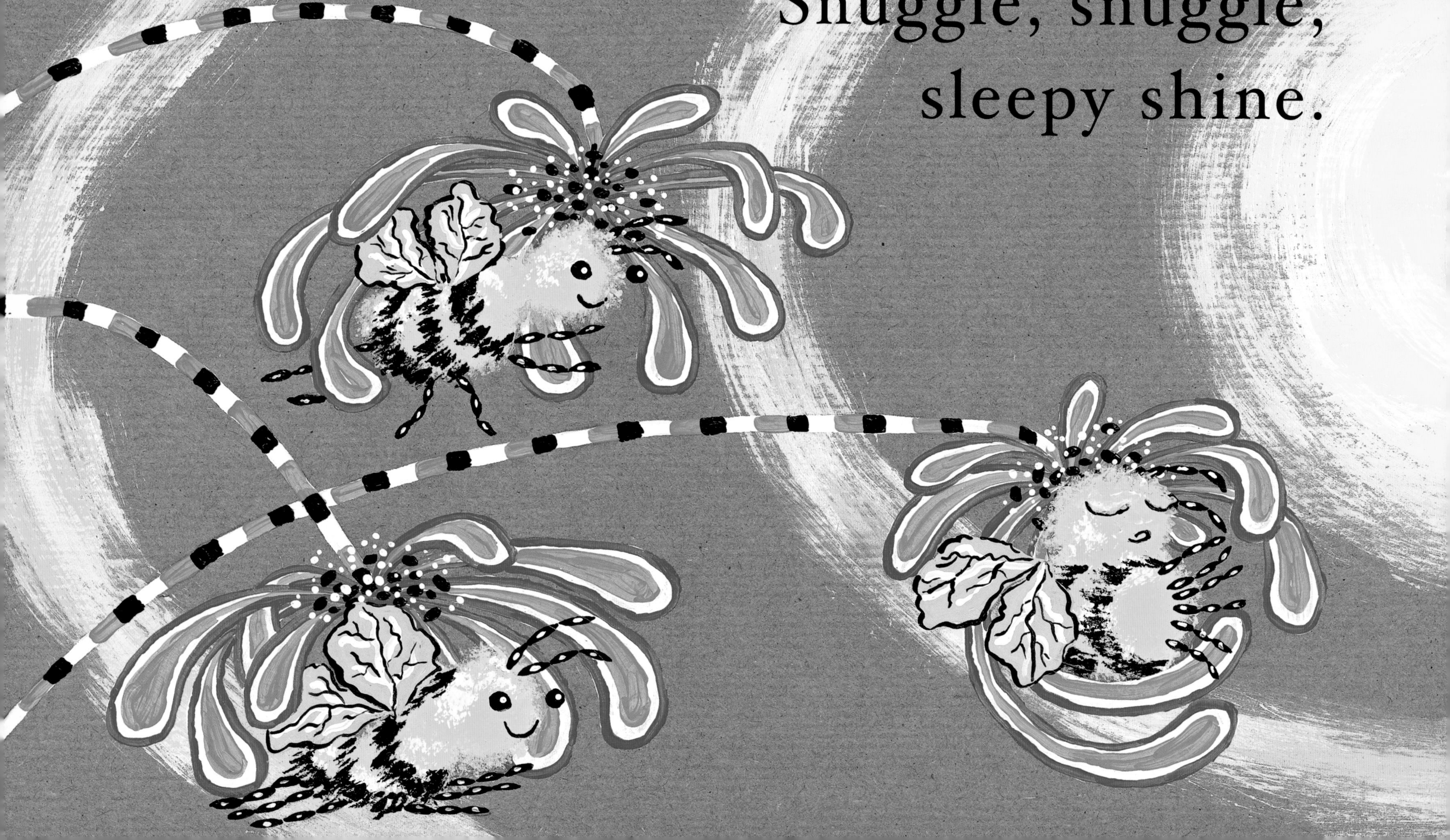

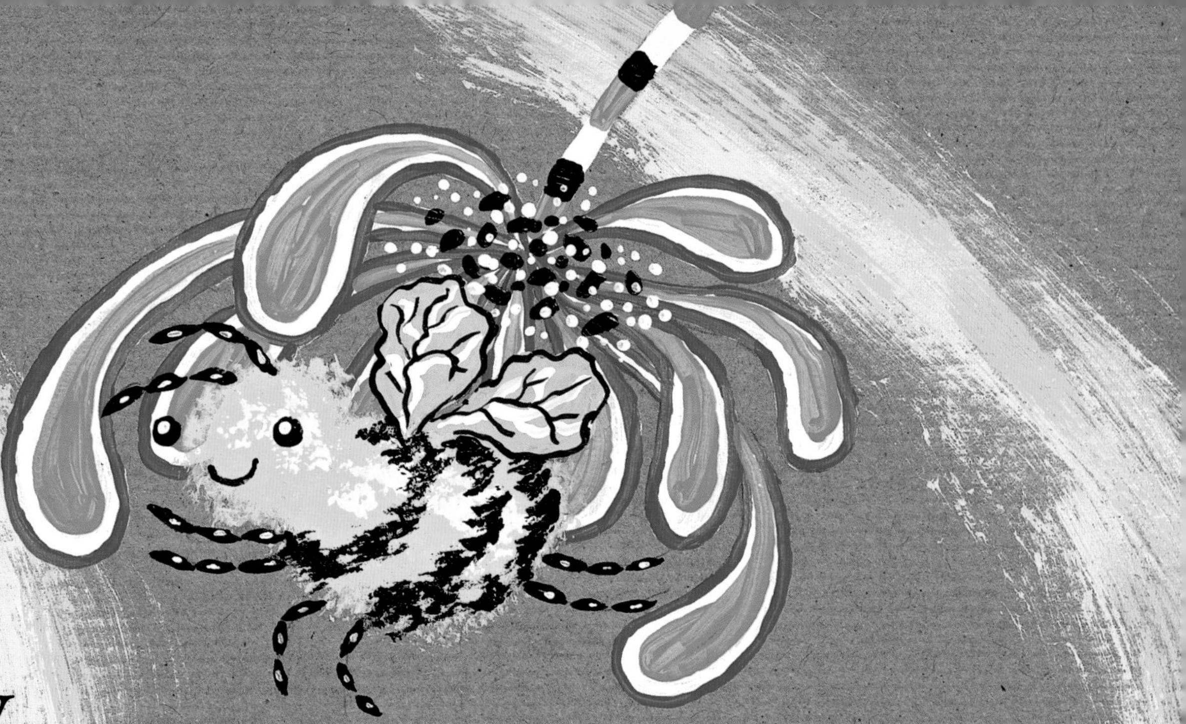

Lazy...dozy.
Snoozy...woooooozy.

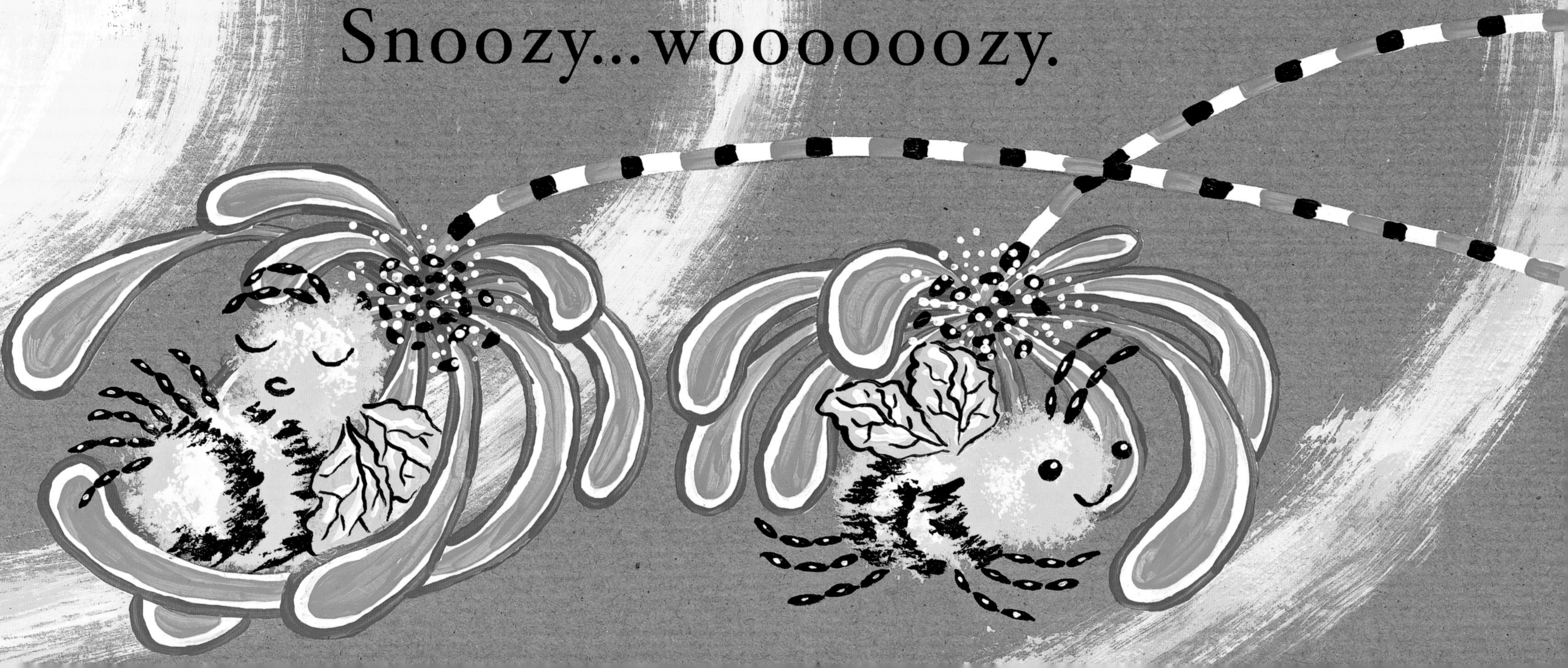

Sleep...sleep. Sleeep...sleeeeeeep.
Ever so quiet.
Not a peep.

Then...

Pitter, patter.
Pit. Pit. Patter.

Splitter, splatter.
Wet. Wet. Wetter.

CRASH!

BANG!

WALLOP!

What on earth

was that?

Sticky, icky chicky.
Soggy, groggy moggy.

Wet. Wet. Wet.

Crazy...
dizzy...
buzzer!
How will we get DRY?

Sunny, sunny breeze and shine.

Fluff and fur and fuzz.

Sunny, sunny blow and shine,

f-f-fluff and f-f-fur and f-f-fuzz.

Cooler.
Quieter.
Late. Late. Later.
No more skit.
No more scatter.

But what about tomorrow?
Now... that's another matter!

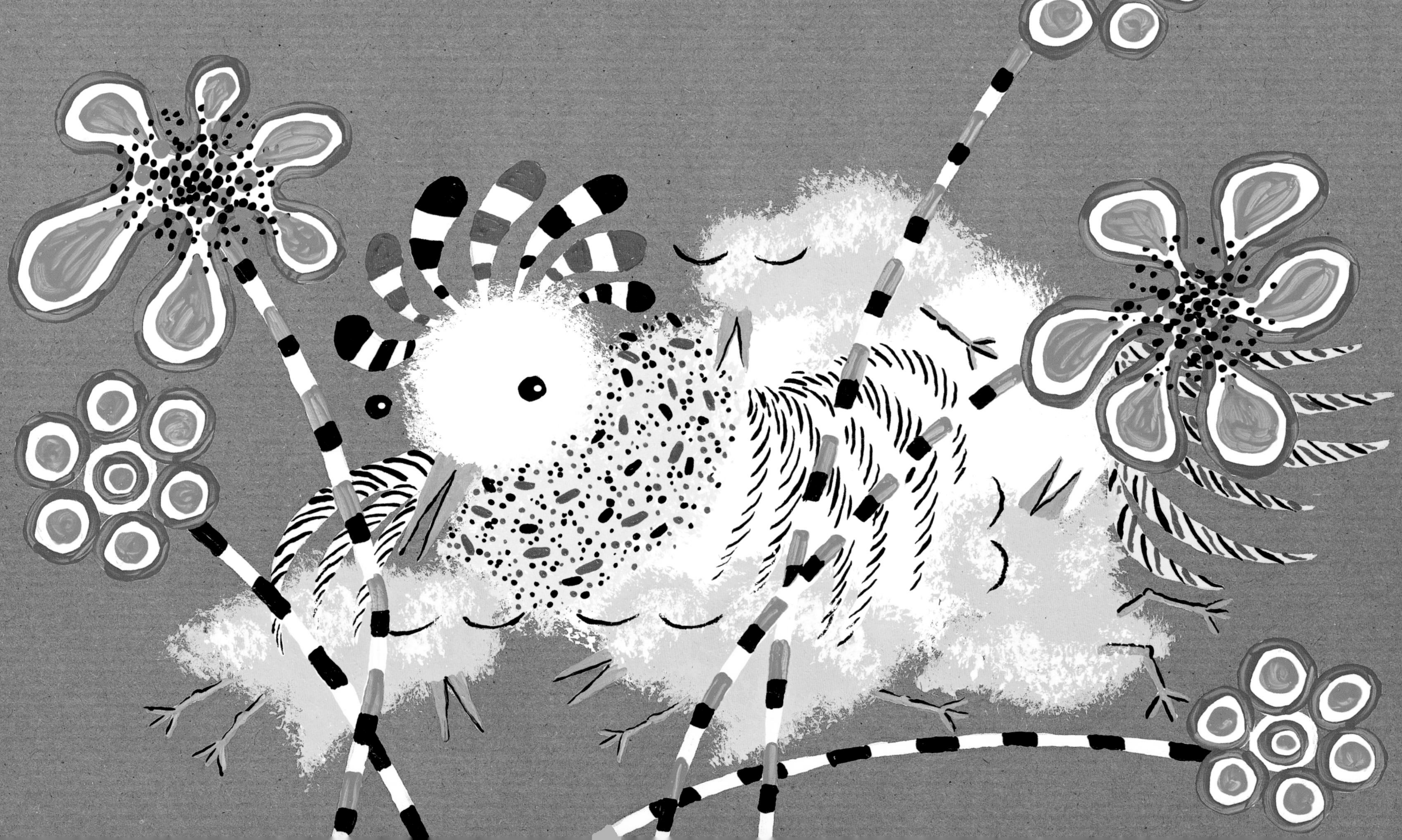